Girls Got Game

girls' **VOLLEYBALL**

Setting Up Success

by Heather E. Schwartz

Consultant
Peggy Miranda, Administrator
The Volleyball Institute of America

Capstone
press
Mankato, Minnesota

Snap Books are published by Capstone Press,
151 Good Counsel Drive, P.O. Box 669, Mankato, Minnesota 56002.
www.capstonepress.com

Library of Congress Cataloging-in-Publication Data
Schwartz, Heather E.
    Girls' volleyball : setting up success / Heather E. Schwartz.
    p. cm.—(Snap books. Girls got game)
    Summary: "Describes volleyball, the skills needed for it, and ways to
compete"—Provided by publisher.
    Includes bibliographical references and index.
    ISBN-13: 978-0-7368-6826-6 (hardcover)
    ISBN-10: 0-7368-6826-7 (hardcover)
    1. Volleyball for girls—Juvenile literature. I. Title. II. Series.
GV1015.4.W66S35 2007
796.325082—dc22   2006021507

Editor: Becky Viaene
Designer: Bobbi J. Wyss
Illustrator: Kyle Grenz
Photo Researcher: Charlene Deyle

Photo Credits:
Capstone Press/Karon Dubke, 5, 9, 10, 12, 13, 15, 19, 20–21, 23;
Comstock Klips, backcover, 4; Corbis/Cathrine Wessel, 7; Corbis/Reuters, 27;
Corbis/Reuters/Jorge Silva, cover; Getty Images Inc./Andy Lyons, 29;
Getty Images Inc./Bongarts/Alexander Hassenstein, 26; Getty Images Inc./
Reportage/Donald Miralle, 25; Getty Images Inc./Stephen Shugerman, 28;
Hot Shots Photo, 32; PhotoEdit Inc./Jeff Greenberg, 16–17

1 2 3 4 5 6 12 11 10 09 08 07

TABLE OF CONTENTS

CHAPTER ONE

GET SET

Do you have a take-charge attitude? Are you strong, powerful, and maybe even a little aggressive? Say yes, and you fit the description of a great volleyball player. Take Elisabeth Bachman, for example. She says she was one of the worst players on her team when she started playing volleyball in 7th grade. In 2004, she was part of the Olympic U.S. Women's National Volleyball Team.

The moral of her story: getting better at volleyball takes determination. Even if you aren't so sure of yourself on the court now, keep practicing. Start today, and you could be on your way to playing like a pro.

So What Is Volleyball Anyway?

Do you like to be surrounded by a circle of friends? Indoor volleyball teams have six players.

Are you more of a one-on-one type girl? Beach volleyball teams are a partnership of two. Playing beach volleyball means extra challenges, like adjusting to wind and sun.

Both types of volleyball use the same skills: passing, setting, spiking, serving, and blocking. Whether you choose indoor or beach volleyball, you'll need to focus on teamwork.

Volleyball players work as a team. One player serves the ball over the net. On the other side of the net, players work together to return the ball in three or fewer hits. The two teams volley until the ball drops to the ground or one team hits the ball outside of the court lines. Whichever team wins this rally scores a point. Your goal is to be the first team to win 25 points, called a set. But the match doesn't end after one set. Stay strong, because you'll need to play three or five sets.

Keeping Score

Ready to pass, set, and spike your way to victory? Volleyball is scored in two ways. Most teams use rally scoring. In rally scoring, a team scores when the other team doesn't return the ball inside the court in three or fewer hits. The team that wins the rally gets one point and the right to serve. The first team to earn 25 points wins the set.

The other type of scoring is called side out. In side out scoring, a set is won by the first team to earn 15 points. With this type of scoring, teams can only win points when they are serving. For both types of scoring, teams play either three or five sets and need to win each set by two points.

Faults

A team gets a chance to serve or continue serving when the other team commits a fault. Examples of faults include:
- Touching the net
- One person hitting the ball twice in a row
- Crossing over the center line
- Hitting the ball with your palm and lifting it into the air

"Play as much as you can. Just as practicing and fine tuning the specific skills in the game are essential to your growth, putting them all together and actually playing games is hugely important.

—Kerri Walsh
U.S. Women's Beach Volleyball player

CHAPTER TWO

HITTING THE COURT

Each indoor volleyball team has six players on the court at one time. Players are divided into a front and a back row by the attack line. Players rotate throughout the match, so you'll get a chance to play all the positions. No matter which position you're in, you'll need to know the five basic volleyball skills.

Serving

This move gets the match started. A powerful serve is tough to return. Careful aim is also important. Many young and beginning players start with the underhand serve. More experienced players get better accuracy and speed by using an overhand serve. Players can only serve from behind the line in the serving area.

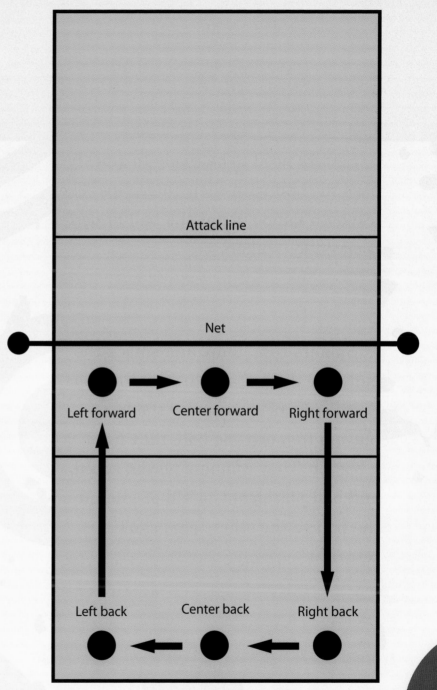

Attack line

Net

Left forward Center forward Right forward

Left back Center back Right back

Serving Area

Setting

Setters need to be ready to quickly pass the ball with their fingertips. They use both hands to put the ball in perfect position for spikers.

Spiking

Spikers run, jump, and smack the ball over the net and toward the floor. Since spikers are usually the last players to touch the ball, they have a big job. They combine power, speed, and ball placement to kill or ground the ball so the other team can't return it.

Blocking

One, two, or even three players may work together to stop the other team from scoring. These front row players jump straight up and raise their hands to block the ball. They usually use this skill to stop a spike.

Picture Perfect

Think professional volleyball players wait until they're on the court to get pumped? Not a chance. They visualize perfect plays before the match begins. Try this before your next match. It's hard to fail when you can't even imagine playing poorly.

13

Passing

Unless your team has already hit the ball twice, it's a good idea to pass to a teammate. That way, you can work together to plan a winning hit. Passers stand in the back row and are usually first to hit the other team's serve. Their goal is to pass the ball to the setters or spikers in the front row.

Call the Ball

No matter what position you play, it's important to call the ball. Yell "Got it!" or "Mine!" when you're going for the ball. Then your teammates will know you're getting the ball, so you don't crash into each other. You can also help your teammates by calling the ball in or out if it's near the boundary lines.

CHAPTER THREE

GET IN THE GAME

Many girls play their first volleyball match in gym class. You probably won't get the chance to join a school team until you're in middle school. But even if you don't play on a school team, you can start playing volleyball now. Join a community team through an organization such the U.S. Youth Volleyball League. These teams are located all over the country for kids ages 8 to 14. They are based on age, not ability.

Some volleyball players prefer a sandy surface to an indoor court. The Amateur Athletic Union (AAU) and the United States Volleyball Association (USVBA) host beach volleyball tournaments for kids nationwide. To find a partner and get some practice, find a beach volleyball program in your area.

School Teams Rule!

In 6th or 7th grade, many girls have a chance to start playing volleyball for their school and compete against other schools. Making the team may not be easy. Work on improving your speed, balance, control, strength, and confidence before tryouts.

As your game improves, try out for your school's junior varsity or varsity teams. What a great way to show school spirit while doing something you enjoy!

Pressure-Free Play

Competitive volleyball isn't the only way to play. You can join a community volleyball league. Everyone makes the team. You still play to win, but your school's reputation doesn't ride on the final score. Community leagues don't lead to the Olympics, but they're lots of fun.

Challenge Yourself

Want to bump your volleyball game to the next level? Improve your volleyball skills at a volleyball camp. Tryouts to be part of elite High Performance camps are held all over the country.

High Performance teams are your next step after camp. USA Volleyball runs a High Performance program that sets girls on the path to the top. Younger players are part of the Youth National Team. After that, the Junior National Team takes players through college. Don't worry—you won't have to quit your school team to play. High Performance tournaments take place during the summer.

CHAPTER FOUR

BECOMING THE BEST

Practicing serves, blocks, sets, passes, and spikes will improve your game. But even the best skills aren't good enough without proper sleeping, stretching, and exercising.

Getting ready for the volleyball season to start? A few weeks beforehand, get your body ready by hurdle jumping, stair climbing, and biking.

During the season, start match day out right by getting 8 to 9 hours of sleep the night before. When you're well-rested, you'll be ready to serve up your best match.

Stretching is a good way to get your muscles ready to play. Spend about 10 to 15 minutes stretching before a match or practice.

Going Pro

Playing professional volleyball is an option for top players. Most go pro after graduating from college. The Association of Volleyball Professionals (AVP) holds beach volleyball events throughout the United States. The best professional players also use their skills at the next level—the Olympics.

Keep working and developing the skills that can make you a standout player. Eventually, you could even play on the U.S. Women's National Volleyball Team. Coaches for this team scout national tournaments and college teams for star players. They invite outstanding players to try out for the national team.

Why Wait?

Guess what? You don't have to be college age or older to play in the Olympics. The best players on high school teams attract attention. If your coach thinks you have a shot, he or she can work to get you an invitation to try out for the U.S. Women's National Volleyball Team.

“

The entire Olympics
experience was
surreal. It's hard
to put in words. It
was an incredible
journey.
—Elisabeth Bachman
U.S. Women's National
Volleyball Team member

”

CHAPTER FIVE

PRO PLAYERS

From hardwood floors to sandy courts, professional volleyball players make the sport look simple. But it isn't easy. Hard work and dedication have helped these famous females reach success.

Ever dream of getting in a match with one of your favorite volleyball players? It happened for Kerri Walsh. When Walsh was in high school, she asked her sports hero for an autograph. A few years later, that same player, Misty May-Treanor, was Walsh's partner in beach volleyball. Between 2003 and 2004, May-Treanor and Walsh won 15 major international titles. And they were also 2004 Olympic champions.

Misty May-Treanor and Kerri Walsh

Tara Cross-Battle

Only the best players are asked to represent the U.S. Women's National Volleyball Team at the Olympics. Tara Cross-Battle's outstanding skills earned her a spot on the U.S. Olympic Team in 1992, 1996, 2000, and 2004. She is the first U.S. volleyball player to compete four times in the Olympics. Cross-Battle retired from her long career after the 2004 Olympics. Today, her love of the game has her coaching at a junior volleyball club in Houston, Texas, called the Texas Tornados.

Gabrielle Reece

Gabrielle Reece got tons of attention when she played pro beach volleyball in the 1990s. Everyone noticed her height of more than 6 feet (1.8 meters), her beauty, and of course, her athletic abilities. And Reece doesn't shy away from showing her skills and strengths. Her advice for other strong, tall girls: "Don't worry about towering over the guys. Stand up straight." Reece also reminds girls to eat right. She says, "You can't build muscle without food."

Some people told Tayyiba Haneef she'd never be a star volleyball player. But her commitment and hard work paid off. Today, she's a member of the U.S. Women's National Volleyball Team. Haneef's next goal? She'd love to win an Olympic gold medal one day. Haneef says, "I believe that as long as you want to do it, and your heart is willing to put forth the effort, anything is possible."

Tayyiba Haneef

Just think—one day, you could be the star athlete encouraging young volleyball players. Stay in the game and always believe in yourself. You can do it!

GLOSSARY

block (BLOK)—an attempt by one or more front row players to stop a spiked ball before, just as, or after it crosses the net

pass (PASS)—bumping the ball up and off the forearms

rally (RAL-ee)—a back-and-forth exchange of the ball between two teams

serve (SURV)—the first hit to start off a rally; serves are aimed at the other team's side of the net.

set (SET)—using the fingertips to direct the ball to a player who can spike it across the net

spike (SPIKE)—a forceful hit made by a player to gain a point; a spike is also called a bury, hammer, or kill.

FAST FACTS

- Volleyball was invented in 1895 when William G. Morgan combined basketball, baseball, tennis, and handball.

- Indoor volleyball was added to the Olympics in 1964, but beach volleyball wasn't added until 1996.

- The Volleyball Hall of Fame in Holyoke, Massachusetts opened in 1987. Players celebrated with a two-day volleyball tournament.

- More than 30,000 spectators came to watch the Girls' Volleyball Junior Olympics in 2004.

READ MORE

Balcavage, Dynise. *Gabrielle Reece.* Women Who Win. Philadelphia: Chelsea House, 2001.

Ditchfield, Christin. *Volleyball.* A True Book. New York: Children's Press, 2003.

Fauchald, Nick. *Bump! Set! Spike! You Can Play Volleyball.* Game Day. Minneapolis: Picture Window Books, 2006.

INTERNET SITES

FactHound offers a safe, fun way to find Internet sites related to this book. All of the sites on FactHound have been researched by our staff.

Here's how:

1. Visit *www.facthound.com*

2. Choose your grade level.

3. Type in this book ID **0736868267** for age-appropriate sites. You may also browse subjects by clicking on letters, or by clicking on pictures and words.

4. Click on the **Fetch It** button.

Facthound will fetch the best sites for you!

ABOUT THE AUTHOR

Heather E. Schwartz loved volleyball in college, but she wasn't really ready for competitive play. Instead of trying out for the school team, she formed an intramural team with her friends. The experience was so rewarding, she continued playing just for fun after graduation.

These days, Heather works as a freelance writer for kid-friendly publications, such as *National Geographic Kids*. She especially likes working on articles about sports, fitness, and health. She also teaches workshops for girls through Girls Inc., a national non-profit youth organization.

INDEX